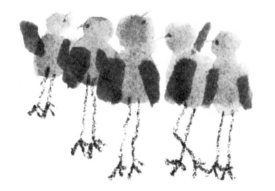

ARTHUR

by Rhoda Levine

illustrated by Everett Aison

The New York Review
Children's Collection, New York

THIS IS A NEW YORK REVIEW BOOK
PUBLISHED BY THE NEW YORK REVIEW OF BOOKS
435 Hudson Street, New York, NY 10014
www.nyrb.com

Library of Congress Cataloging-in-Publication Data

Levine, Rhoda.
  Arthur / by Rhoda Levine ; illustrated by Everett Aison.
    pages cm — (New York Review children's collection)
  Summary: When Arthur misses the chance to migrate with the other birds, he
discovers a winter wonderland in New York City.
  ISBN 978-1-59017-935-2 (hardback)
 [1. Birds—Fiction. 2. Winter—Fiction. 3. Christmas—Fiction. 4. New York
(N.Y.)—Fiction.] I. Aison, Everett, illustrator. II. Title.
  PZ7.L5785Ar 2015
  [E]—dc23
                              2015016481

ISBN 978-1-59017-935-2
Available as an electronic book; ISBN 978-1-59017-942-0

Cover design by Louise Fili Ltd.

Printed in the United States on acid-free paper.
10 9 8 7 6 5 4 3 2 1

FOR MY MOTHER AND FATHER

It has been a fine lush summer in New York.
All the birds agreed that Central Park
had never been greener.
With the coming of autumn, however, they
knew they must go south for the winter. All
such birds go south for the winter.

When the time came to fly away, the birds counted their
number. Someone was missing! Arthur was not there!
"Really," all the birds croaked, "why must
Arthur be so . . . 'inconvenient.' He is never
around when important moves are being made."

At that moment, Arthur was riding
through the park. He was gazing
at himself in the taillight of a hansom cab.
He was enjoying himself immensely!

The birds began to search for him.
"The time has come, Arthur," they chattered,
"to fly south to a warmer climate."

But Arthur could not hear them. He
had left the cab and was perched
on the prow of a rowboat. He was looking
into the lake, dreaming of wider seas!

All the birds grew tired.

"Maybe Arthur does not want to go South," one bird suggested.

"Not go!" the other birds cried in amazement.
"Why any bird worthy of the name goes South for the winter."

Arthur heard none of this. Now he was enjoying
the sound of a calliope as he rode around
on the wooden ear of a carousel pony.

The birds grew exhausted. They huddled together to rest.

"Maybe Arthur has decided to stay here for the winter,"
another bird ventured. "He is such an odd bird,
such a strange bird, such a very private bird.
This is the kind of decision he would make."

All the birds nodded. This must be the answer.
Suddenly a gust of wind blew up. It lifted the birds
off the ground. It was a strong wind indeed!
It lifted them higher and higher into the air.
They were on their way. There was no turning back.

The birds looked down for one final look.
And then they saw Arthur. He was far below them,
peering at himself in a puddle.

"Last chance to join the crowd, Arthur," the
birds chirped as the wind drove them on.

Arthur did not move. He was taking a drink.
He was lost in thought.

Arthur preened a feather.

"I could do with a game of hide and seek," he said suddenly. "I think I'll find a friend to play with."

A cool wind chilled him as he started in search of a playmate. "Feels like autumn," he said to himself. "I'd best suggest to all the birds that the time has come to fly to a warmer climate."

Arthur searched for an hour. He looked all about him. But hard as he tried, he could not find a friend.

Arthur began to feel uneasy. Where could all the birds be? You don't suppose..., he thought. He dared not think on. But when another hour passed, he had to admit it. The birds had gone South without him.

Arthur shook himself. "I have long been curious about New York in the time that is not summer," he said. "It might be an adventure to stay." Yet his heart sank slightly, and he felt a little left alone.

"I shall take courage and toss my head
proudly," he said. He tossed his head back,
but he was still worried.
"Time to whistle a tune," he said. Arthur
listened to his song. "What fine tone!"
he exclaimed. "These chilly winds may
do wonders for my voice."

His song finished, he flew off to his nest.
But when he got there, he found that
the winds had blown his nest into
a hundred scattered pieces. For the first time
he noticed that all the trees stood bare.
"Something has happened to the trees,"
he said. "It is most peculiar. Surely the
leaves will grow back again tomorrow."
Arthur chuckled carelessly. But he was not at ease.

Happily he found one leaf that still clung
to a branch. He huddled behind it. It
would serve as shelter for the night.
"There is nothing like a good dependable leaf,"
he said aloud.

Early next morning, Arthur
awoke shivering. His dependable leaf had joined the others.
It lay on the ground.

I'm in need of a real home,
he thought; a place I can
count on.

He found a dried acorn and
had breakfast.

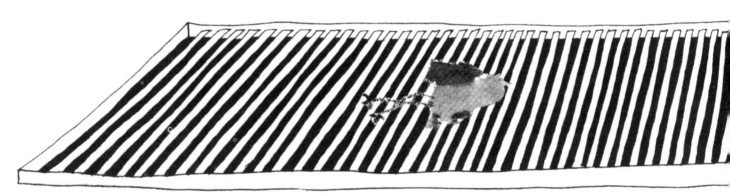

Then he flew off in search of a new
home. Everyone in the city was
still asleep.

"I am an early bird," Arthur said.
Suddenly he saw what seemed to be
the perfect solution to his housing
problem. Arthur discovered a warm
metal grate in the middle of a
midtown sidewalk.

"This is a fine location for a home,"
Arthur chirped as he settled down.
Warm air rose from the grate.
Arthur dozed.

It was almost nine in the morning when he was rudely awakened. He found himself trapped among running boots, galoshes, shoes, and rubbers. His heart stopped. He rose quickly into the air.

There must be a fire somewhere, he concluded. But he saw no smoke.

At last the grate was free of feet, save for one or two passers-by. Arthur settled down again to enjoy the grate's warmth. Once more, however, as evening approached he was roused by those same boots, galoshes, shoes, and rubbers running in the opposite direction.

"There must be a foot race in progress," he said.

He felt strengthened in his conclusion when a lagging lady muttered, "Rush hour," and took to a taxi.

The next day the races occurred just as before, one in the morning and one in the evening. Arthur flew to a traffic light before they began. He tried to pick a winner on one occasion. He chose a man with glasses and whistled and chirped encouragement to him. But with all Arthur's urging, it seemed to him that no one really won. The only thing accomplished was a great deal of push and shove.

How odd all this is, Arthur thought.

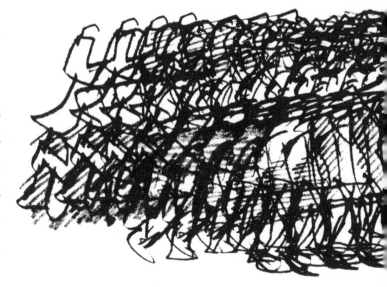

Two days passed. The sun had gone
on vacation. The wind was sharper. The air
was colder. Arthur made an observation.

"New Yorkers are changing shape," he
said. Everyone was wrapped in hats and
coats and scarves. Children tottered
as they waddled about in bulky outfits.
Everyone hunched against the winds.

"People can be entertaining," Arthur
commented as he watched the world
walk by. "I am growing. I am learning.
I am an acute observer."

Arthur, too, hunched against the cold
when he left his warm grate. He had
to be more and more away from it.
Breakfasts, lunches, and dinners were
becoming harder and harder to find.

Arthur thought of consulting the pigeons about this problem. They always looked fit and well fed. But he felt, after all, that they did not speak the same language.

One morning when there was not a seed, an acorn, or a worm to be dug up anywhere, Arthur sat sadly on the back of a park bench. He was very hungry.

"This situation is not funny," Arthur said. "I am feeling very fragile, indeed."

Suddenly he heard a most unbirdlike whistle. Arthur cocked his head. As he did so, a spray of soft white crumbs fell all around him. The spray had come from the hand of an old man who stood nearby. The man was smiling.

"This certainly looks like an invitation to me," Arthur murmured. Without a moment's hesitation, he devoured all the crumbs in sight. "Here is a man whose hand understands a bird," Arthur said to himself.

This breakfast was the first of daily breakfasts that Arthur enjoyed that winter. For the man with the generous hand was at the bench to greet him each morning; and each morning, Arthur feasted.

"New York is a pretty fine place when it comes to bread crumbs," Arthur declared each day.

"Subway grates are fine for a while," said
Arthur one well-fed morning. "But flitting
from grate to street lamp twice a day
is not my idea of real comfort. I must find
a home without interruptions."

So Arthur devoted himself to house hunting.
The weather was cold. But Arthur persisted.

"It may be cold," Arthur said to himself,
"but I am strong in heart."

Days passed. Arthur's strong heart grew
faint. Pigeons roosted everywhere, and they
did not seem inclined to move over. Arthur
perched finally on the head of a statue
in the park one afternoon. He was exhausted.

"It is to the pigeon's credit," he declared, "that
they are so wise when it comes to housing;
but I do wish they were more eager to share."

Arthur looked down at his feet. They were so cold he could hardly stand up.

"Maybe if I stand on my head," he said, "I shall be able to think more clearly."

From this new view, Arthur discovered a wonderful thing. The statue held a book that might be as useful to a bird as it was to a statue.

Quickly he turned himself right side up. He collected blades of dried grass from around the statue's foot and arranged them tastefully in the statue's book. He nestled among the grass. "Most comfortable this," he said. Arthur had found a permanent home.

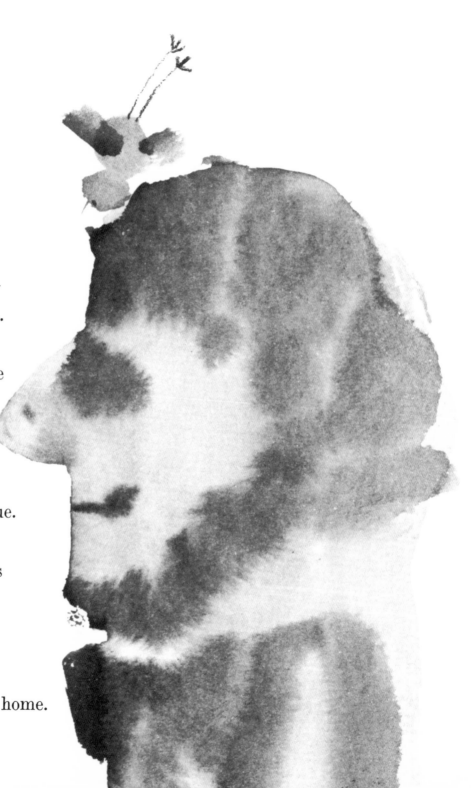

Yet, as the days wore on, Arthur felt
strangely uneasy. Housed and fed
as I am, he thought, I do need a little
recreation. He pondered a game
of hide and seek. But there was no place
to hide and no one to seek.

"I cannot go gameless an entire
winter!" Arthur finally declared. "I
must look for something to do."

One evening during his search he saw
a strange, misty spot in the street.
Arthur approached the spot. Here it
was that he finally found his game.
Arthur had discovered the "steaming manhole cover."

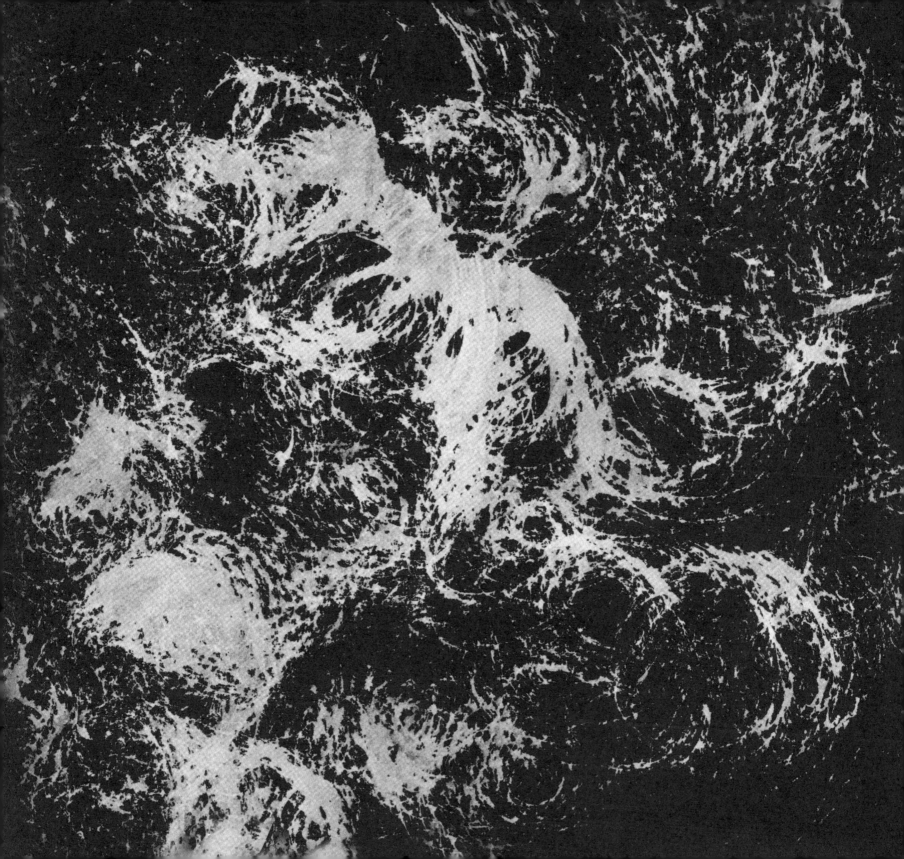

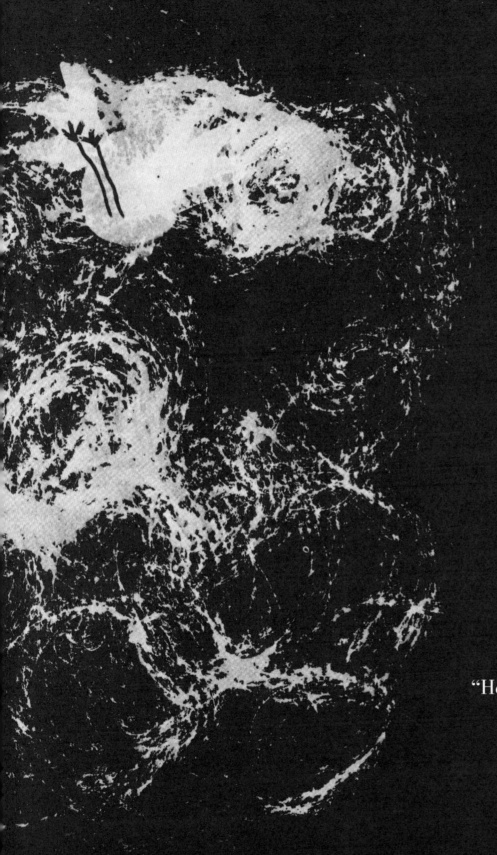

Now he could play hide and seek.
But since he had no companion, he
had to call the game "Find Arthur."

It could best be played in the
evening. Then the street was free
of cars and the steam was at its
best. The game was played
by strict rules. First Arthur took a
deep breath and advanced on the
manhole cover. He then took
three one-legged hops and landed
smack in the center of the cover.
He lost himself in the steam.

"Where is Arthur?" he would cry.

Then turning himself round and
round, and counting to seven, he
would take one big hop and
emerge from the mist.

"Here I am!" he would chirp with delight.
Arthur had found a sport that
even a private bird could play.

Days of flying and feasting and fun followed
for Arthur. New York surely is a fine place
to be in winter, he decided.

Yet one night Arthur felt unnerved. He was
awakened by a most curious sound. His statue
seemed to ring and ping. A hard icy rain was
falling. It fell through the whole, long night.

The next morning when Arthur awoke, the
trees were sheathed in ice. The ground was
wet and cold below him, and something
glistened and gleamed before his eyes.

"What can this be?" Arthur asked as he
looked at the shiny point that hung before him.
"It looks like water, yet it hangs in the air."

Gazing at it, Arthur forgot about breakfast.
Arthur forgot about everything. He looked
at the shiny surface the whole day long.

"If I were good at naming things," Arthur
said finally, "I should call this an *icicle*."

Suddenly he felt fired to poetry.

"Icicle, Icicle,
I'd like to ride a bicycle."

Arthur languished in these lines.

I may be a poet, he thought.
He pondered this for several days.

Then one morning Arthur began to
hear new sounds. Bells rang out with
great frequency. People began to sing.

Arthur saw a group of New Yorkers
gather to sing "Gloria" on a terribly
cold night.

"Surely the world wants to be a
bird," Arthur said as he sat on his
statue's finger. The world might make
a very good bird, indeed, he reflected.

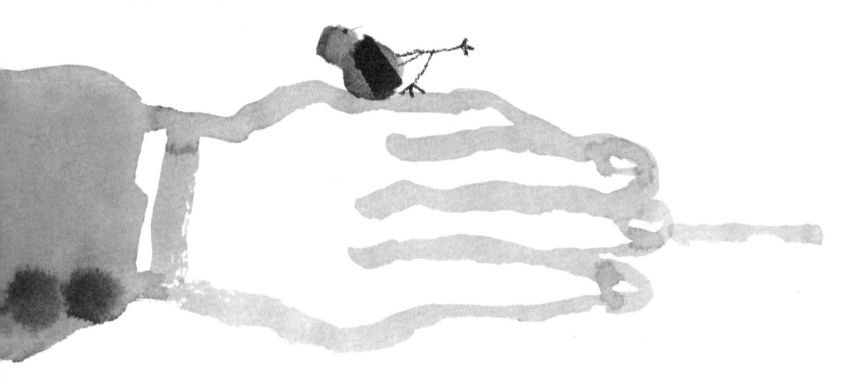

During this time of song, Arthur had
a strange and happy surprise.
A huge evergreen tree appeared
suddenly in a public square not far
from Arthur's nest. It was the
biggest tree he had ever seen.

"Well, that's a fast growing tree,"
Arthur declared in amazement. "I am delighted to see
so much green once again."

So great was his joy that Arthur
decided to go on vacation. He would
spend a few days among the green boughs.

The next day he flew to the tree.
Arthur looked out on the world
through a lacework of green twigs.
The odor of pine was lovely.
He felt happy. He felt contented.
But that night as he settled down
to sleep, an unforgettable thing
happened. The tree did something
shocking! It did not whisper in
the wind. It did not lose its
greenery. It did, however, light up!

Arthur was dazzled. Arthur was frazzled. Arthur was terrified. Arthur swallowed a big swallow. But he could not leave. He was held by the bright colors that blazed before him.

"I've never heard of such a tree," Arthur said. "It must be a new variety."

"Look at the Christmas tree," someone shouted from below.

I guess this is a Christmas tree, thought Arthur. He remained there for several days.

But on the fourth day he left. The dazzle had become too much for him to bear.

During the week that followed he often returned to enjoy the sight of the tree. One day, however, when he got to the square, he found that the tree had disappeared.

Strange tree, Arthur thought. I am learning many new things. I have really set sail on a great sea of discovery and exploration. I am truly an admirable bird.

The next morning Arthur the discoverer, Arthur the explorer, opened his eyes. He promptly closed them again. Then he opened them very slowly. The brilliance he had seen the first time was still before him. Though Arthur had discovered many surprising things, no surprise was as great as this.

A white blanket lay humped and
piled over everything in sight. Could
this be the New York he had known
in the green of summer? The city
was silent, except for the sounds of
shovels scraping and children
shouting. There was not a car to be
seen. Arthur felt some hesitation
about leaving his nest.

"Courage and humor, Arthur," he
said to himself. "The children aren't
afraid. The children are laughing."

Arthur flew off through the wondrous
white park to his breakfast place.
The hand was there to greet him.

Once in flight Arthur enjoyed
the day, although he could not
bring himself to touch the white
stuff. He flew and hovered
above the park until he was quite
exhausted. He felt he could
hover no longer. He must land.
He closed his eyes and plunged.

He landed and opened his eyes.
The ground was fearfully cold.
Arthur jumped back into the
air at once. But as he jumped,
he looked down. He saw, to his
delight, that his footprints
remained below.

Immediately he set about
hopping up and down in the
snow. Once he did a somersault
and landed on one foot!

"I feel I am a dancer," he sang.
To finish his footprint pattern
with a touch of elegance, he flew
an S curve and landed beak
first. Arthur sneezed.

"This is really for the birds,"
he said.

The day of dancing footprints tired him. That night Arthur did not even mind that his nest was cold. He fell asleep quickly.

The next morning, Arthur turned a phrase. "New York is a winter wonderland," he said. He had every reason to feel this. For in the days that followed, he saw strange and wonderful things.

Once he saw children slide down hills on their bellies. Looks like fun, Arthur thought. I think I'll try it myself.

So he did. He found a snow-covered rock and belly-slid from top to bottom.

"Good game," Arthur sang after this first trip. "It even beats a carousel ride."

Another day Arthur found the air filled with snowballs. Arthur declared a race between the balls and himself. But snowballs proved poor competition. They always fell to earth.

"White balls are low on flying power," Arthur declared; and he turned to watching other things.

Sometimes he sat on a curb and watched car wheels as they spun and tossed snow into the air. He preferred them to the wheels that were chained and moved slowly.

"Spinning car wheels are fun," Arthur said. "And spinning people are more fun." He moved to the lakeside to watch the skaters whirl on ice.

But the thing that brought greatest joy to Arthur was the sight of people who slithered and slid about on the soft white ground. Arthur tried sliding about and falling over, himself. It amused him no end. He giggled himself into a state of sheer exhaustion.

Enough of this, he thought at the end of a slippery day. And he took to the air in a dizzy flight home.

The snows went, and came and went again. Finally Arthur awoke one morning to find a warm breeze blowing. People who walked beneath his statue seemed to feel it, too. Their coats flapped open. They walked slowly. They had lost their winter hunch.

Arthur flew among tree branches and saw small green buds.

"I feel suddenly light in heart," he said to himself.

But that night the weather was cold as ever.

"Can one ever trust Mother Nature?" Arthur asked woefully before he fell asleep.

After that the days really did grow
warmer. They seemed longer than
those that had gone before. Tree buds
began to swell. One day Arthur
brought a large bud to the man who
fed him. One good turn deserves
another, Arthur thought as he made
his presentation. The old man smiled.

Warm days continued. There was
much rain. Puddles became plentiful.

One morning Arthur was considering
himself in a particularly fine puddle
when he heard loud chirping in the
air above him. He looked up.
The birds had returned.

"Arthur," all the birds chattered, "is that really you?"
They landed. "Yes," they agreed, "it is the same
old Arthur, puddle and all."

Arthur thought. Then he said quietly, "No, I am not
the same Arthur at all. I am a bird who has played
in the mist, danced in the snow, written a poem, and
feasted on crumbs each day. I am a bird who has lived
through a strange and a cold and a wonderful time."

The birds could not really listen. They were too full
of their southern adventures. They gleefully chattered
and chirped and flapped about on the grass.

"You don't look well, Arthur," commented a chubby
bird finally. "Not well at all. What a pity you could not
be with us. Think what joy you missed."

Arthur, still peering
happily into his puddle,
thought, I had best be a
modest bird and not talk
of all that I have seen. Such
tales can wait for another day.
The birds chattered on and on.
When they grew tired, they
looked once more toward the
puddle. But Arthur was not there!
Arthur was riding the roads of
Central Park. He was gazing at himself in the taillight of a hansom cab.
He was enjoying himself immensely!

RHODA LEVINE is the author of seven children's books and is an accomplished director and choreographer. In addition to working for major opera houses in the United States and Europe, she has choreographed shows on and off Broadway, and in London's West End. Among the world premieres she has directed are *Der Kaiser von Atlantis* by Viktor Ullmann and *X—The Life and Times of Malcolm X* and *Wakonda's Dream*, both by Anthony Davis. In Cape Town she directed the South African premiere of *Porgy and Bess* in 1996, and she premiered the New York City Opera productions of Janáček's *From the House of the Dead*, Zimmermann's *Die Soldaten*, and Adamo's *Little Women*. The New York Review Children's Collection publishes her books *Three Ladies Beside the Sea* and *He Was There from the Day We Moved In*, both illustrated by Edward Gorey.

Levine has taught acting and improvisation at the Yale School of Drama, the Curtis Institute of Music, and Northwestern University, and is currently on the faculty of the Manhattan School of Music and the Mannes College of Music. She lives in New York, where she is the artistic director of the city's only improvisational opera company, Play It by Ear.

EVERETT AISON is a co-founder of the School of Visual Arts Film School in New York and the former art director of Grossman Publishers. He has written several produced screenplays and designed the opening titles for numerous films, including Akira Kurosawa's *Yojimbo* and Roman Polanski's *Knife in the Water*. In addition to *Arthur* he has illustrated the children's book *The American Movie* and in 2006 published his first novel, *Artrage*.

TITLES IN THE NEW YORK REVIEW CHILDREN'S COLLECTION

ESTHER AVERILL
Captains of the City Streets
The Hotel Cat
Jenny and the Cat Club
Jenny Goes to Sea
Jenny's Birthday Book
Jenny's Moonlight Adventure
The School for Cats

JAMES CLOYD BOWMAN
Pecos Bill: The Greatest Cowboy of All Time

PALMER BROWN
Beyond the Pawpaw Trees
Cheerful
Hickory
The Silver Nutmeg
Something for Christmas

SHEILA BURNFORD
Bel Ria: Dog of War

DINO BUZZATI
The Bears' Famous Invasion of Sicily

MARY CHASE
Loretta Mason Potts

CARLO COLLODI and FULVIO TESTA
Pinocchio

INGRI and EDGAR PARIN D'AULAIRE
D'Aulaires' Book of Animals
D'Aulaires' Book of Norse Myths
D'Aulaires' Book of Trolls
Foxie: The Singing Dog
The Terrible Troll-Bird
Too Big
The Two Cars

EILÍS DILLON
The Island of Horses
The Lost Island

ELEANOR FARJEON
The Little Bookroom

PENELOPE FARMER
Charlotte Sometimes

PAUL GALLICO
The Abandoned

LEON GARFIELD
The Complete Bostock and Harris
Smith: The Story of a Pickpocket

RUMER GODDEN
An Episode of Sparrows
The Mousewife

MARIA GRIPE and HARALD GRIPE
The Glassblower's Children

LUCRETIA P. HALE
The Peterkin Papers

RUSSELL and LILLIAN HOBAN
The Sorely Trying Day

RUTH KRAUSS and MARC SIMONT
The Backward Day

DOROTHY KUNHARDT
Junket Is Nice
Now Open the Box

MUNRO LEAF and ROBERT LAWSON
Wee Gillis

RHODA LEVINE and EVERETT AISON
Arthur

RHODA LEVINE and EDWARD GOREY
He Was There from the Day We Moved In
Three Ladies Beside the Sea